D1208926

The United States

Washington

Paul Joseph
ABDO & Daughters

visit us at
www.abdopub.com

Published by Abdo & Daughters, 4940 Viking Drive, Suite 622, Edina, Minnesota 55435. Copyright © 1998 by Abdo Consulting Group, Inc., Pentagon Tower, P.O. Box 36036, Minneapolis, Minnesota 55435 USA. International copyrights reserved in all countries. No part of this book may be reproduced in any form without written permission from the publisher.

Printed in the United States.

Photo credits: Cheryl Goehrs, AP/Wide World Photos, SuperStock, Archive Photos, Corbis-Bettmann

Edited by Lori Kinstad Pupeza
Contributing editor Brooke Henderson
Special thanks to our Checkerboard Kids—Brandon Isakson, Francesca Tuminelly, Stephanie McKenna

State population statistics taken from the 2000 census, city population statistics taken from the 1990 census; U.S. Census Bureau.

Library of Congress Cataloging-in-Publication Data

Joseph, Paul, 1970-
      Washington / Paul Joseph.
      p. cm. -- (United States)
      Includes index.
      Summary: Examines the geography, history, natural resources, people, and sports of the Evergreen State.
      ISBN 1-56239-895-4
      1. Washington (State)--Juvenile literature. [1. Washington (state)] I. Title. II. Series: United States (Series)
      F891.3.J67   1998
      979.7--dc21

                                     97-31414
                                     CIP
                                     AC

Contents

Welcome to Washington

The state of Washington lies in the northwest corner of the United States. This area is also known as the North Pacific Region. Cape Alava, an area in Washington, is the most western part of the continental United States.

Washington is a very pretty state and it attracts many visitors. For every one person that lives in the state, there are two people that are visiting. **Tourists** are attracted to the state's unbelievable beauty.

Washington has scenic mountains, clear lakes and rivers, splendid cities, and wonderful weather. It also has 157 miles (253 km) of beautiful coastline.

Half of the state is covered in thick forests. That is how Washington got the nickname the Evergreen State. The rich land in Washington is excellent for farming. Washington is also known for its many parks.

Ruby Beach in the state of Washington.

Fun Facts

WASHINGTON

Capital
Olympia (33,840 people)
Area
66,512 square miles
(172,265 sq km)
Population
5,894,121 people
Rank: 15th
Statehood
November 11, 1889
(42nd state admitted)
Principal rivers
Columbia River
Snake River
Highest point
Mount Rainier;
14,410 feet (4,392 m)
Largest city
Seattle (516,259 people)
Motto
Alki (By and By)
Song
"Washington, My Home"
Famous People
Bing Crosby, William O.
Douglas, Mary McCarthy, Dixie
Lee Ray

*S*tate Flag

*R*hododendron

*W*illow Goldfinch

*W*estern Hemlock

About Washington

The Evergreen State

Detail area

Washington's
abbreviation

Borders: west (Pacific Ocean), north (Canada), east
(Idaho), south (Oregon)

Nature's Treasures

The tallest part of Washington is the Cascade Range. The Cascade Range is a towering chain of mountains that stretches straight down the middle of the whole state. There are four peaks in this range that tower more than 10,000 feet (3,048 m). There are other mountain ranges in the state, too.

The Evergreen State has more than 23 million acres of forest land. Douglas fir and western hemlock trees are seen the most in the forests.

The rich farmland in Washington ranks among the top 10 states in the amount of **crops** grown. Washington has many fruit trees. The state grows a lot of apples, pears, and other fruits. Flower farmers grow fields of tulips and daffodils.

The Pacific Ocean and many lakes and rivers offer boating, fishing, rafting, and water sports. The volcano, Mount St. Helens, is an awesome sight that attracts millions of visitors each year. In 1980, the volcano began to erupt after lying **dormant** since 1857.

A girl playing in a tulip field.

Beginnings

The first known people to live in what is now Washington were **Native Americans**. Some of the Native Americans included the Chinook, the Nez Percé, and the Yakima.

The first European **settlers** in the Washington area were fur traders and trappers. Most of them were from England. Both England and United States claimed the Washington region in 1792. In 1818, the United States and England agreed to share this area together.

Both countries lived in Washington until 1844. By this time the United States and England were fighting over the land. In 1846, England agreed to give the entire area to the United States.

In 1853, the northwestern area of the U.S. was called the Washington Territory. Olympia was named the state capital. For the next 30 years the **population** remained very low. The people of this area, however, wanted to become a state.

In 1867, the Washington Territory asked for statehood. But congress said that they needed a constitution before they could be a state. The state leaders finished it in 1878. Finally, on November 11, 1889, Washington became a state. It was the 42nd state.

A woodsman on horseback packing through the Washington Territory.

1818 to 1889

Owners to Statehood

 1818: The United States and England agree to share the area.

 1819: Spain gives up claim to what is now Washington.

 1846: England gives up the region so the United States owns the entire area.

 1889: Washington becomes the 42nd state on November 11.

Washington

1818 to 1889

1931 to Now

Modern Day Washington

1931: The Rock Island Dam on Columbia River is completed.

1950: The Tacoma Narrows Bridge is finished.

1980: Mount St. Helens erupts, causing $2.7 billion in damages and kills 60 people.

1989: The state of Washington celebrates its centennial—100 years of statehood.

1996: Gary Locke is the first Chinese-American ever elected as a state **governor**.

Washington

1931 to Now

Washington's People

There are five million people living in the state of Washington. It is the 15th most populated state in the country. The first known group of people to live in the area were **Native Americans**.

Today, many well-known people have come from Washington. The great NFL quarterback John Elway was from Port Angeles, Washington. Elway was drafted by the Baltimore Colts, and later the Denver Broncos and baseball's New York Yankees. He chose to play football and led the Broncos to a Super Bowl victory.

William Boeing started the Boeing Airplane Company in Seattle. His company made airplanes and fighter planes for the United States Army.

Chester Carlson was born in Seattle. He was an inventor who came up with the idea for a copy machine. After noticing that people sometimes needed many copies of one document, he came up with xerography. He named his company the Xerox Corporation.

Dixie Lee Ray was the **governor** of Washington from 1977 to 1981. She was only the second American woman to be elected as a governor in the United States.

William Boeing

John Elway

Dixie Lee Ray

Splendid Cities

Washington has many splendid cities in its state with many things to do and see. People from Washington live in both large and small cities. Only three cities have more than 100,000 people.

The largest city in Washington is Seattle. Just over 500,000 people live there. Seattle is a major port city on the Puget Sound. It is known for its many **industries**.

Seattle's most famous business is Microsoft. The richest man in the world, Bill Gates, owns Microsoft. The city is also known for its scenic beauty, the Naval Air Base, museums, the Seattle Aquarium, and the Woodland Park Zoo.

Spokane has nearly 200,000 people. It is located on the far eastern side of the state, near

20

the **border** of Idaho. Spokane has many colleges in the city.

Tacoma is the third largest city in Washington. This city makes airplanes, things made out of wood, and electronics. Tacoma also has the Point Defiance Park Zoo.

Washington's state capital is Olympia. Other splendid cities are Bellevue, Everett, Yakima, Bellingham, and Walla Walla.

The Seattle skyline.

Washington's Land

Washington has some of the most beautiful land in the country. Its land is divided into seven different regions. The Olympic Mountains region covers the northwestern part of the state. This mountainous area is mostly wilderness.

In the southwestern corner of the state is the Willapa Hills region. These hills follow the coast down to Oregon and northern California. The Puget Sound Trough region crosses the state from north to south in the western side of the state. This has bays, inlets, rivers, and valleys.

The Cascade Range runs through the middle of the

state from north to south. This mountainous region has four peaks that tower more than 10,000 feet (3,000 m).

The Columbia Plateau region covers almost the entire mid to southeastern part of the state. This area receives little rainfall.

In the northeastern part of the state is the Okanogan Highlands region. This area connects the Rocky Mountains and the Cascade Range.

The Blue Mountains region is in a very tiny area in the southeastern corner of Washington. This region reaches into Oregon, with its mountains rising from 2,000 to 4,000 feet (600 to 1,200 m).

Mount Rainier, in Washington.

Washington at Play

One of the **tourist** attractions in Washington is Mount St. Helens National Volcanic Monument. This volcano began erupting in 1980 after lying **dormant** since 1857. Another awesome site is the highest point in the state, Mount Rainier.

Washington's incredible mountains offer some of the best climbing and skiing in the country. It is also fun to just stare at the tall mountains and take pictures.

Washington has ski **resorts**, golf resorts, and fishing resorts. Many people fish off the coast of Washington or in the many lakes and rivers. People also enjoy other water sports like boating, water skiing, and swimming.

The many cities in the state offer fun things to do too. Seattle is the most visited city in the state. The Seattle Seafair features parades, boat races, and water carnivals.

Inside people can watch their favorite professional sports teams thanks to the Seattle Kingdome. Three sports teams play in Seattle: baseball's Mariners, football's Seahawks, and basketball's SuperSonics. The Sonics play in the Seattle Coliseum.

People in Washington enjoy the ocean, rivers, and lakes.

Washington at Work

The people of Washington must work to make money. Many people work in large cities while others work in small towns. Some people work on small farms in **rural** areas while others work in tall skyscrapers.

A lot of people in Washington work in some kind of **manufacturing**. Some people build ships and airplanes. Many people work for the Boeing Company, which makes airplanes.

Because of the many forests in Washington, the trees provide a lot of wood to make things, like furniture. Some companies make machines or computers. Many people in the state work for Microsoft. Some people work at Nintendo. Nintendo makes video games for kids.

Many people farm in Washington. There are about 38,000 farms there, with many different kinds of **crops** grown. Farmers grow wheat, fruits, and green peas to name a few.

Because Washington's coast is on the ocean, many people in the state fish in big boats in the ocean. Some of the fish that are caught and sold around the country are salmon, shrimp, and cod.

Washington offers many different things to do and see. Because of its natural beauty, people, land, coast, and cities, the Evergreen State is a great place to visit, live, work, and play.

People playing a computer game at Nintendo headquarters in Redmond, Washington.

Fun Facts

- The first name for the state of Washington was going to be Columbia. In 1853, however, it was changed to honor the first president of the United States, George Washington. Washington is the only state named after a president.

- Mount Rainier, the highest point in Washington, is the snowiest place in America.

- The Evergreen State has many trees. In fact, the state of Washington grows many of the Christmas trees that people put in their houses in December.

- Many people visit the Seattle Aquarium to study fish. The Aquarium has a 400,000-gallon (1,514,000-liter) underwater viewing dome. It is one of the largest in the world.

- There are only a few rain forests in North America. Some of them are in Washington. Most places in this continent are too cold and dry for rain forests.

The Quinalt Rain Forest in Washington.

Glossary

Agriculture: another name for farming.

Border: neighboring states, countries, or waters.

Crops: the plants that farmers grow on their land, like corn, beans, or cotton.

Dormant: a temporary hold on growing, moving, or other types of activities.

Governor: the highest elected official in the state.

Industry: many different types of businesses.

Manufacture: to make things by machine in a factory.

Native Americans: the first people who were born in and occupied North America.

Population: the number of people living in a certain place.

Resort: a place to vacation that has fun things to do.

Rural: outside of the city.

Settlers: people that move to a new land where no one has lived before and build a community.

Tourists: people who travel for pleasure.

Internet Sites

Washington State Historical Center
http://www.wshs.org/index2.htm
A very colorful and interactive site about education, museums, publications, and much more.

Mount Baker Snowboarding
http://www.nas.com/baker/report.html
This is a fun and exciting site all about snowboarding in Washington state.

These sites are subject to change. Go to your favorite search engine and type in Washington for more sites.

PASS IT ON

Tell Others Something Special About Your State

To educate readers around the country, pass on interesting tips, places to see, history, and little-known facts about the state you live in. We want to hear from you!

To get posted on ABDO & Daughters website, E-mail us at "mystate@abdopub.com"

Index